HER SECRET BILLIONAIRE

BAD BOY BILLIONAIRES - BOOK 3

JESSA JAMES

Her Secret Billionaire
Copyright © 2017 by Jessa James as Lumberjacked

All Rights Reserved. No part of this book may be reproduced or transmitted in any form or by any means, electrical, digital or mechanical including but not limited to photocopying, recording, scanning or by any type of data storage and retrieval system without express, written permission from the author.

Published by Jessa James
James, Jessa
Her Secret Billionaire

Cover design copyright 2020 by Jessa James, Author
Images/Photo Credit: VitalikRadko; 4045qd; Ssilver

This book was previously published as Lumberjacked.

GET A FREE BOOK!

Join my mailing list to be the first to know of new releases, free books, special prices and other author giveaways.

http://freehotcontemporary.com

1

nna

"I will be so pissed if I die delivering this jerk his groceries," I muttered to myself as I gripped the joystick and tried to ignore the bouncing of my old floatplane.

That was impossible since the last drop had my stomach relocating in my throat. The sky had turned a nasty dark gray twenty minutes ago, the kind that didn't bode well for me, the only pilot crazy enough to go out flying in my dad's twenty year old tin can of an airplane.

I should be on the ground with my face in a textbook, but Jack-ass Buchanan, the spoiled city slicker, had his groceries delivered every week and I wasn't going to shirk my job. I was the lucky one—not—who kept him from starving to death. Since he lived out in the bush, nearly two hours from Anchorage by plane, it's not like he could pop into the city to pick stuff up. There was a small fishing village about a thirty minute drive from his place, but I delivered there, too.

Another rollercoaster dip made the plane shudder and I fought to stay on course.

The man, Jack, or Jack-ass as I thought of him, just oozed money. Old money. Silver-spoon money. I had no idea why he quit the city and came up to Alaska. Most people who came up here did it for one of two reasons. One, they had the wilds in their blood. Jack Buchanan was handsome and rugged, had muscles to die for, but he didn't exactly fit in with the rugged lumberjack crowd that frequented the local bars all summer. And since living out in nature wasn't in his blood, that left option two...the rest of them came up here to hide. From the law. From an ex. Whatever. It didn't really matter, but I knew how much people out in the bush depended on deliveries like mine. And I wasn't about to let the man starve. Which meant I got the unlucky job of visiting him once a week.

If I could just look my fill and leave, that would be fine. But as with most people up here, he didn't get much company. When he did, he liked to come out to the plane, say hi, chat me up for as long as it took me to unload.

Despite long months of weekly conversations, I didn't know much about him other than the fact he was somewhere over thirty, tall, tan, drop-dead gorgeous and liked S'mores flavored PopTarts. Not that I'd ever admit to him that he was hot as hell. His clothes always fit a little too well to be from the local co-op, even if they were the rugged look that everyone in the area wore. He had one of those Grecian noses with cheekbones that made me want to rub my face on his like a cat. While he was pretty low key about the fact that we were two of the only youngish, single people in the area, I saw how his chocolate brown eyes wandered to my breasts and my ass, when I unloaded his groceries every week.

I'd be lying if I said my eyes didn't wander, too. I figured I owed it to women everywhere to check him out, to take careful note of the bulge of his pecs under his flannel shirts, the veins that ran up his forearms, the tanned skin on the back of his neck. His dark, dark brown hair was getting longer each week—he needed a haircut. Either that, or he needed to let my fingers run through the unruly locks. I wanted to tug that hair, wanted to rip that flannel shirt off him. Wanted to climb him like a goddamn tree and have him press me up against the wall of his cabin and fuck me until I couldn't breathe.

He'd be good, too. I had no doubt he knew just how to get a woman to beg for more.

Yeah, thoughts of him wielding his cock like a weapon were working well to distract myself from the choppy skies that bounced me around my cockpit seat. I shook myself out of my fantasy sex reverie and took a quick glance at the dashboard. The pressure had built around the cockpit, a sign that the turbulence was only going to get worse.

Don't think about it, just fly, I heard my dad's voice in my head.

He'd taught me to fly when I was just a kid. Since I was old enough to buckle my own straps I flew with him on his runs when I wasn't in school, even learned to do my homework in the co-pilot's seat without getting plane sick. I got my pilot's license the day I turned eighteen and we had a party at the hangar. Now that he was gone, I'd taken over his routes, his plane, everything. His business became mine. Flying was what I loved and I was really fucking good at it. But these storms were always a bitch. They were rough when one was on the ground. In the air....

The plane dropped a good ten feet and I gritted my teeth and held on to the throttle with both hands.

It was time to leave Alaska. Past time. I wasn't wild. I loved the mountains and the forests, but I had as much of my city-girl mother in me as my outdoorsy father. I didn't want to hide from life up here. I wanted to *live* it. I wanted to see the world. Explore everywhere. I wanted to visit every country I could, taste every exotic food. I wanted to see the bright lights of New York and hear the eerie howl of the coyote in the Arizona desert at night. I read every night, made lists of places I wanted to go. I was only twenty-four, but my bucket list was two pages long. None of which I could do stuck up here in Podunk Alaska with the bears and the lumberjacks.

After Dad died last year, I knew it was time to go. I was fucking sick of the cold, sick of the dark, sick of delivering other people's groceries. I wanted to be somewhere else, somewhere I could still fly but make more money doing it. I was so ready to get the hell out of here and my dad's old house was the only thing stopping me. I couldn't quite afford to set off on my own without the money from the house, but I didn't exactly live in a town with a hopping real estate market. So I waited. And I studied. I had one semester left of my online college classes to go. When I got out of here, I'd have both my pilot's license, and a business degree.

A gust came from the east and buffeted the plane.

I kept my head down, remained focused on the instruments, the plane, the sound of the wind. There as in instinct to flying that not everyone understood. I'd tried to explain it to some of my dad's old buddies in town, but they'd just laughed...at both of us. There were days I would swear the wind whispered to me. Days I knew where it was going to blow, knew a storm was coming despite the radar. Weather was crazy up here, could turn on a dime, and this storm was proof of that. It was supposed to be ninety miles south of me for another few hours. More than long enough for me to get in, drop of sex-on-a-stick's grocery order and get back.

I was so close to getting out of here. Even if Buchanan decided he wanted to start something, I'd have to tell him no thanks. I had goals. I had plans. And a new man didn't fit into them. At least not one from up here.

That meant avoiding men until I could get out of this place, especially hot ones with dark eyes and unkempt hair. Now was not the time to be distracted. I'd worked the last few years to get ready and I was leaving for the lower forty-eight. Falling for someone was the last thing I needed.

So, of course, my thoughts wandered to Jack-ass and how I wanted him to tug down my jeans, push me over the railing of his deck and take me from behind.

No. No. NO!

"Stop that." I scolded myself aloud, but knew it wouldn't help.

I forced my thoughts back to the future. I could not fall for someone, especially not some stupid city-slicker who'd be starving by now if it wasn't for me. I needed a real man, one who could handle me.

So, falling in love was out of the question. But what if Jack just wanted hot monkey sex?

I continued to monitor the console, check the altimeter. Jack would probably be a fun fuck buddy—how could he not, with muscles and a face like that? I smiled to myself, as I thought about the hot sex we could have. One night might be perfect. Just enough to take the edge off my need, give my vibrator a little vacation.

Just one night, I could do that, I kept telling myself, even though the rational part of my brain scoffed loudly. *Yeah, right, Anna.* I had just started to roll my eyes at myself when the plane lurched so roughly I let out a yelp. Shit, this storm was nasty. *Time to get out of the damn sky.*

My elevation was decreasing with the intense turbulence, something that never boded well for a floatplane. Jack's house was right on a lake with no room cleared through the trees for an actual *land* landing. Water landings were all I could do in this plane anyway. I loved to watch the floaters cut through the choppy gray waves, but in this weather, water landings —or any landings for that matter—were brutal.

Still, any landing was a good landing. Hell of a lot better than the alternative...

I forced myself back into automatic pilot mode.

Dad had taught me to fly "technical," so I kept to what I knew and met each problem with calm. The wind shook the entire body of my little cargo plane and I knew the landing was going to be bad.

God, hope Jack doesn't see this. He already thinks I'm incompetent.

I didn't know why I cared, but that seemed important to me—that he didn't watch me struggle to land sideways on the water. If I wanted to keep my job, my clients, I needed to be seen as a strong, independent woman who flew like a badass. Alaska was huge in land but small on people. One bad word from him at the closest fishing village and the news would spread. Until the house sold, I needed to keep flying to pay the bills.

As I watched my radar, I knew I was only about a mile out from my usual landing spot. I continued to decrease my altitude as I worried that doing so would drop me from the sky like a stone. In this wind, who knew what the airstreams would be like? I gripped the joystick tighter as I turned a little west, then a little north, then a little east to get a feel for the airstream. Landing on the water would be much easier with the wind at my back, but in this storm, the wind ripped from all directions. Any way I approached, it was going to be bumpy.

I aimed for the landing spot and I zoned in on the last three hundred feet of elevation. I bounced roughly around my seat, thankful for the strong body harness keeping me from hitting my head. My headset flew off after one especially strong gust and I tried to be gentle as I directed the joystick, and the nose of the plane, further down. I couldn't see a damn thing through the rain and the fog on the water, but I knew I was far enough from the shore. Jack's house sat like a beacon of light about a quarter mile from my landing spot and I knew I was right on the nose.

The bumping and bouncing continued as I tried to level out the plane, but it was a lost cause. The tail end was going to hit the water—hard—but it was better than the nose. I'd go through the windshield if I hit the nose. I held onto the joystick with both hands as the wind jostled me just fifty feet above the water. At the last second, I pulled up on the joystick and forced the nose up and the tail down. The tail *smacked* the water, the floaters connected loudly with the waves, and my plane teeter-tottered wildly as it coasted. I continued to coast as the plane slid across the choppy surface of the lake, my floaters rocking for a moment long before they settled.

Holy shit.

I breathed out as I decelerated the plane and turned towards the massive dock by the shore. The wind was even more intense on the water than it was in the air and I had to accelerate more than usual to get to the spot where I turned off the engine. The plane coasted the last fifty feet or so.

That was going to make a great story when I get back to town, I thought, but then balked as I realized I wasn't flying home until the weather cleared. Until then, I was stuck out here. With Jack.

2

ack

Where the hell was she?

Anna Jackson was a wisp of a woman, but she was a force to be reckoned with. All five foot nothing of her and she flew a damn floatplane. She was the Alaskan version of FedEx and I relied on her for all my deliveries, even my fucking groceries.

How did such a tiny woman command that damn plane? And in this shitty weather. As I looked outside, a hard rock of worry settled in my gut as I realized that she just might be ballsy enough to risk the damn delivery.

It was near dark, but not because of the sunset. The sky had turned a nasty, dark gray, and the wind was so bad that the trees looked like they were growing sideways. At this time of year, the sun set around midnight and it was barely seven. She wasn't late, but it was *dark* and with this storm, I couldn't imagine a worse time to be in a small plane. I'd heard that bush plane crash rates were higher than any other. No wonder, with the crazy ass weather. She was probably already on her way when the weather changed. But had she turned back?

Moving inside, I picked up my radio and tried to call through to the nearest village, get them to radio Anchorage and find out if she was on her way or sitting safe and sound at home. On good days, I could get a clear signal. Today, there was no answer, as I'd expected with this damn storm. I tried my computer, but with the cloud coverage, my satellite service was down as well. No way to get messages in our out until the storm cleared.

I sat down at my desk and flipped through the pages of my cousins' small tech company's investor portfolio to keep from worrying. She was a big girl. Knew what she was doing. Knew my supply of spaghetti sauce and toilet paper weren't worth dying for. No. She was safe on the ground, waiting out the storm.

I returned to the details of Buchanan Technology.

My cousins had started it two years ago and had grown the firm exponentially, which I'd expected. I'd been involved in my own business then and watched from across town as they'd taken built it from the ground up. Everyone said the Buchanan's had a head for business. Since they heard I'd sold my company—the deal was big enough to make it through the business circles and of course through the family—they wanted me to join them. But I'd sold and walked. I wasn't ready to return to the real world, to the fucking rat race and I'd told it to every headhunting cold caller since. If I did decide to get back into tech—I wasn't hurting for cash—Natalie and Ben's company would be my first choice. A return to Seattle was a big deal, though, and I wasn't going to rush into a decision. I'd left the city, and all the bullshit behind for a reason. That reason hadn't changed. Maybe I would be ready tomorrow, maybe I needed a little more time.

Speaking of time. I looked out the window, watched the rain paint my window sideways.

Work wasn't effective as a distraction. I kept thinking about Anna, the infuriating woman with her shit kicker boots, tight jeans, and perfect breasts she tried so damn hard to hide under those long sleeved shirts that clung to every curve. She was stubborn as hell and every week she refused to let me help her unload her plane. Always said she didn't want me to fuck up my manicure.

Oh honey, I wanted to purr in her ear, *You're the only thing I want to fuck...*

I never got close enough to say it; she never seemed interested and I wouldn't fuck a woman who wasn't willing. I'd be lying if I said her reaction to me didn't sting a little. Women had wanted me my entire life, practically thrown themselves at my feet, but that was only because they knew I was rich. That's why Victoria had pretended to fall in love with me. I let it happen, too. I'd even been the dumb-ass who'd asked her to marry me.

I shook the thoughts off, not wanting to go there. It had been over a year ago since the shit storm that became my life once I learned Victoria had been lying to me. Over a year since I moved to Alaska. I loved the unspoiled vistas, the rugged people, the quiet. This time of year, mid-August, the weather was warm, the days were long and near perfect. I spent hours hiking and exploring the woods, some days the breeze was chilly enough for a jacket, but the daylight lasted almost twenty hours.

My mom came to visit about a month after I settled in. Even she loved my little house, the lake, the wind in the trees and the wild animals that made their way to the water's edge to drink. She hadn't stayed long, just long enough to make sure I was all right, and long enough to find Anna. My mother insisted that I needed human contact and fresh food, so she hired Anna's company to make deliveries once a week. I was pretty sure Mother did it because she thought Anna was beautiful and secretly hoped I'd fall for her. The irony was not lost on me.

Anna was beautiful and curvy in all the right places. She was honest and hard-working and tough as nails. Could I fall for Anna? Probably. But Anna didn't give a shit about me, my money, any of it. Each week she left me with my deliveries and a hard on that seemed to be focused entirely on her.

As I paced the floor, I occasionally checked the window over my kitchen sink and stared out towards the dock. The storm had picked up so much that I couldn't see that far out; the rain and wind had made the usually stunning view gray. But then I saw it. Her plane, a ghostly orb, about fifty feet up from the water. The streak of white in the gray sky stuck out like a sore thumb, but so did the position of her plane. *Holy shit, she's going to nosedive!* I barely spared a thought before I ran out the door, the rain and wind slapping me back as soon as I stepped onto the porch.

I didn't care, though. She was about to crash her damn plane and I already knew I'd do anything I had to to save her. Even jump into the freezing water cold lake and pull her ass out of that damn plane.

As I hauled my body full-speed towards the dock, I watched as she pulled the nose of her plane up at the last possible second.

Calm down, Top Gun, I thought, even as I felt a swell of appreciation in my chest. The butt of the plane smacked hard enough for me to hear it from where I stood, still hundreds of feet away.

That had to hurt, I thought as I picked up the pace. Anger surged, pissed off that she'd hop in her plane in a storm like this. My stupid delivery wasn't worth her life.

But she's a total badass, came a voice from the back of my brain, as I pushed my legs to go faster. I suddenly felt stupid about my "incoming heroics"; Anna didn't need me. She could handle this shit all by herself. My cock jumped at the thought, but I kept sprinting. She coasted rather roughly into the dock just as I got to the steps. I leapt down them in my hurry to get to her and nearly slipped off the dock for my efforts. I ran up to her door, ripped it open, grabbed her by both arms and roared, "What the hell were you thinking? You could have died!"

She was pale, paler than I'd ever seen her, and her pupils were dilated to near-black. She breathed in a rapid, disjointed rhythm, clearly affected by the rough landing and storm. I loosened my grip on her arms and lifted my hands to the side of her face, to her neck, the only bit of skin I could reach, and stroked her cold, clammy skin. The rain whipped around me and blasted its way into the cockpit. In seconds, Anna was soaked through. But touching her brought me back to my center and I lifted her face to look up at me, focused on ignoring her full, ripe lips.

"Are you okay? Anna?"

She blinked, slowly, as if in a daze before her eyes grew sharp and filled with fire. "What the hell, Jack? You're soaking the cockpit. My damn console is drenched! Get the hell out of my way." She undid her harness and leapt down from her seat, slammed the cockpit shut, and moved to the rear of the plane. She was drenched in an instant.

Ignoring the weather, she checked the floaters, probably for damage, and then moved to the anchor, which had wrapped itself around one of the floaters. She struggled for a few seconds and nearly fell into the water before I picked her up with barely any effort and moved her aside. Anna called me something rather colorful, but I pretended not to hear her over the wind. In one swift motion, I untangled the chain and watched the anchor drop into the water.

I turned to her and saw she had opened the cargo hold to pull out coolers.

She's still trying to deliver my damn groceries!

I moved to jerk her away from the plane. "Get your ass inside, you idiot! In case you hadn't noticed, there's a wicked storm and you're soaked. Let's move!" I was inches away from her face as I shouted and I saw her chin jut out in defiance.

"I'm here to deliver your shit, Jack! I'm not letting it

all spoil because of some bad weather." She angled around me to reach for the cooler but I blocked her. I shoved the cargo hold shut, twisted the handle to secure the door, and turned back to her.

She was spitting mad, her strawberry blonde hair plastered over her cheeks and forehead. My cock thumped in my soaked jeans and, knowing she'd stand out here in the storm and argue all day, I leaned down, put my shoulder into her belly and tossed her up and over my shoulder.

"Put me down!" she shrieked at me as she tried to wiggle free.

I didn't listen to her protests, just picked up my pace as I hurried toward the house. Her ass bounced next to my face and I could feel her tits as they rubbed against the wet fabric on my back. My dick got harder and I jogged faster. I'd wanted her in my house. I'd fantasized for a long time about getting her inside, stripping her out of her clothes, and...

This wasn't exactly what I'd had in mind.

I got into the house and threw Anna rather ungracefully onto the couch before heading out to get the two coolers full of food I knew were for me. No telling how long we might be stuck here, and I didn't want to risk even that small amount of food rotting.

When I had everything put away, I returned to find her huddled on the coach, white as a sheet. Her legs were tucked up under her and she was staring into space. I turned to the fireplace and, despite it being August, gathered up wood to start a fire. We were both soaked through and if I was cold, then she was freezing. I also needed time to calm the raging erection that pressed painfully against the front of my soaked jeans. And seeing her body clearly defined by the wet clothes wasn't helping. Nor was the sight of her nipples poking through the fabric of her shirt.

Did she not wear a bra on purpose?

Once the fire roared to life, I heard her fumbling behind me, cursing me as she stood. I smiled to myself, knowing my manhandling had hurt her ego.

"Damn it, I can't stay here. I can't do this," she was talking to herself as she stomped straight for the fucking door. *God, she is stubborn.* I dropped the extra pieces of wood back into the crate and hauled ass to the door, right on her heels. My massive frame loomed over her slender one, my hand over her head kept her from opening the door. It took barely a few seconds to register the fact that my entire torso was pressed against her backside, from ass to shoulders. My pecs pressed nearly into her neck, my erection unmistakable on her lower back. *Shit.*

"You're not flying in this," I said.

"I'm not stupid. Of course I'm not going to fly in this, but I'll sit and wait out the storm in the plane," Anna bit out. She turned to face me and we both realized that was a mistake; my erection pressed into her stomach and we both gasped. She sidestepped the door and I turned my back against it, acting like my dick hadn't just introduced itself.

"Seriously, Jack, let go of the fucking door!" She shoved at me, tried to move me away from the door but ended up slipping in her wet boots. Her ass thumped on the polished wood floor of my cabin and she scrambled up to her knees.

I kind of liked her in that position, kneeling, her full pink lips just inches from my body. So did my dick. Dammit, it wasn't going down anytime soon. Not with thoughts of her fingers working open my jeans and grabbing hold so she could put me in her mouth.

Gripping a wrist, I helped her to her feet. No way could she remain on her knees.

"Sit in the plane, Anna? Really? Why the hell would you want to do that when I have a perfectly good house here with a nice warm fire?"

Of course, with her standing, I got a better view of her hard nipples and I wondered how they'd taste, how they'd feel in my mouth. My knees buckled a bit, the pulse in my cock nearly knocked me over. *Just a hint of her nipples and I lose my fucking mind...* I cleared my throat and tore my eyes away from the fabric that covered her chest.

"I can't stay in here, with you."

"Why not?" Anger rose, real and cold and hard as

fucking steel. "You think I can't keep my hands to myself? Are you afraid of me?"

"No." She shook her head and stepped back, lifting her chin to meet my gaze. "Don't be ridiculous."

"I saw that landing, you almost died." Chastising her was better than imagining her naked if I couldn't touch, couldn't taste.

I threw my arms out wide over the door and met her fiery gaze with my own. She dropped her eyes a bit and blushed, clearly upset I had witnessed her less-than-spectacular landing.

"You weren't supposed to see that," Anna mumbled and turned her back to me. She pooled water on my hardwood with each step, but all I could see was the way her wet jeans clung to her perky, round ass.

"I did and it scared the ever-loving shit out of me. You're staying here tonight. No argument. I'll disable your plane if I have to." Relieved that she appeared to have accepted the fact that I wasn't going to let her go sit in that freezing cold tin can she called an airplane, I moved into the kitchen to grab a towel. She was standing in front of the fireplace when I returned to hand it to her. "Now dry off, you're going to ruin my floor."

She whirled around and looked down at her boots. "You're worried about your floors?" She tossed the towel at me and stomped toward the door. "Forget it. You're impossible. I'll go wait in the plane."

I blocked her path before her third step. "I'm not sure if I should spank your ass for that comment or for being so reckless with your life." The rage flared in me and I stepped closer to Anna, barely a breath away from her face. My eyes pinned her green ones, daring her to mouth off again.

She has no idea who I am.

I'd been the CEO of a multi-million dollar company. Sold it for multi-millions of dollars. No one ever mouthed off to me the way she did. And something about her fire woke me up inside. For the first time since I'd walked away from Victoria and her lies, I felt something other than cold indifference for the world. Apathy melted from me as the fiery red-head before me put her hands on her hips and glared up at me.

"Spank me?"

"Spank you," I repeated, imagining her round ass over my lap. I'd play with her pussy, of course. And not really spank her, not hard. Just enough to make her squirm and pant and beg me for more.

"You are out of your mind, Jack Buchanan."

"Watch what you say to me, Ms. Jackson. You don't know the half of my story, so don't presume that you do."

"So you're the big bad caveman who will spank me for what? Speaking my mind?"

I grinned and lowered my eyes to her lips. "For that

smart mouth, yes. If you were mine, I'd spread you naked over my lap and make you come with one hand while I spanked you with the other." My nostrils flared and I watched as her eyes fluttered to my lips. She took a step back, but she was already too wound up to back down. I saw it in her stance, in the intensity behind her eyes, and my whole body buzzed with adrenaline, with lust, with the need to conquer all that fire and make it mine.

"You're the pretty boy who can't handle your life, running away from the world, hiding out here in the bush. You are a pussy, Jack. And you're afraid of me. Afraid of a woman who lives and takes chances."

"Risking life and limb in that storm wasn't taking a chance, Anna. That was suicide."

"I've been flying since I was old enough to walk. I know what I'm doing."

Every week when she delivered my groceries, Anna brushed off my comments, made jokes about my poorly-cut wood, about my inability to perfect the art of fishing. I wasn't an Alaska boy, born and bred, but damn it, I did well for a Seattle native who had never been this far out in the bush. Her comments fed on that insecurity, on the knowledge that I didn't belong here—or Seattle—or anywhere. So I snapped. I walked forward, stalking her until she was pinned against the wood-paneled wall. "Hmm, no. You have no idea what you are doing."

"Fuck you." Her eyes were glazed and she had her hands in fists at her sides, the knuckles white. Her wet shirt stretched tight over her hard nipples and it was all I could not to lean over and take one of those pert tips into my mouth. I leaned forward just enough to surround myself with the scent of wet rain and woman. Leaning in close, I whispered in her ear, made sure my words were hot and heavy against her flesh.

"No. I think *I'll* fuck *you*."

She swayed toward me in a reaction I wasn't sure she was aware of. In a calculated move, I leaned my body weight against her, my cock pressed against her hip. She gasped and turned to look at me. "I don't understand you, Jack. What do you want from me?"

"I want that smart mouth, princess, all over me. I want to fuck you. Right here, right now."

I thought she'd smack me, *hard,* but instead Anna nearly ripped out my hair in her attempt to pull me into a kiss. It wasn't a chaste peck, it was a kiss filled with months of pent up desire and a shitload of frustration.

Our mouths moved against one another roughly, and I didn't bother to be gentle. I was *feral* and so was she. We took it out on each other like animals; we ripped at clothes, tugged at hair, pinched flesh. We bit each other's lips as our tongues crashed together and finally, finally, I moved my hands down to rip open her flannel shirt, buttons pinging on the wood floor as I pulled the fabric from her body.

Jesus, no bra. Her breasts were perfect, a small handful, upturned and pert with pale pink tips.

"Do you always go without a bra, or just when you fly?" I breathed, raising my hands and cupping the soft globes. Her skin was damp and cool, but wonderfully giving and lush. I wanted to bury my head between them and breathe her in. I wanted to hold them tightly together and rub my cock between them. I wanted to come all over her pale flesh and mark her, own her.

Her eyes closed and her head fell back. I pinched her nipples, eliciting a gasp. "Look at me. I want to see your eyes when I touch you."

Slowly, she opened her eyes, which looked out of focus and a dark, stormy green.

I slid my hands down her waist and undid her jeans, pushing them off her curvy hips. I knelt before her to strip them away. I spent only a second to take in the sight, her pale legs shone in the bright light of my cabin. I reached up and hooked my thumbs in her pink silk panties. Slowly, so slowly, I savored the moment as I pulled them down her thighs. When they were around her ankles I looked up at the body of a goddess as she stood over me. I knelt at her feet and felt something else shake loose inside me, something that I hadn't given free rein in a long time.

I *wanted.*

God, I've wanted this... her, for so long.

I stood and Anna moved forward to unbutton my pants but met the same wet resistance I had with hers. *Note to self, don't wear jeans next time you embark on a rescue mission that could end in angry sex.*

She took part of her frustration, her eagerness, out on my pants, but left angry red marks on my thighs where her nails scraped my legs. I didn't give a shit; I just wanted my dick inside her.

Unwilling to wait, I helped her and removed the rest of my clothes faster than I would have thought possible. As soon as I stepped out of my jeans and boxers, I yanked a condom out of the closest drawer, rolled it on and pressed forward once more. Over her. Around her.

God help me, I wanted to be *inside* her. Lifting my hands I tangled them in her wet, thick locks as her small hands pulled on my hips. She stood on tiptoes to kiss me and I realized how much smaller she was. How far up her belly my cock rested.

She was small, so small I could lift her like a feather and fuck her in any position I wanted.

This was going to be fun.

I shoved her back against the wall, cushioning her head with my huge hand so she wouldn't bang it too hard. I didn't want her to have a headache. I wanted to make her pussy ache. Whole different section of anatomy.

She lifted her lips to mine and we collided again. I lifted her in one swift motion and, as if practiced, she wrapped her legs around my hips. Her pussy nestled right against the heat of my cock and we both groaned loud enough to be heard over the pummeling wind and rain.

Keeping one hand wrapped in her hair, I tilted her head back as I slid the other slowly down her shoulder, over the curve of her waist to her ass. I squeezed her there as I held her in place for my kiss and lowered that hand, wrapping it around her from behind to test her feminine core and slid two fingers inside her in one slow, languid push.

Hot. Wet. So fucking perfect.

"Jack." She whimpered my name, her hips bucking as I worked my fingers inside her. I loved the sound of my name on her lips and I wanted to hear it again. And again. I kissed her jaw. Her neck. Fucked her with my fingers until her thighs tightened and she tried to force my pace, tried to ride my hand.

"You're so fucking wet for me, Anna," I breathed against her neck as I nipped my way up to her ear. I bit down on her lobe and she whimpered. "I want to slide my cock inside you, fill you up. Make you mine."

"Jack, stop talking. Just fuck me." As she attempted to bite my ear in return, her back arched off the wall. The movement shifted her until her wet heat settled on top of my dick, which jerked at the contact.

"Your wish is my command, princess." I took my chance and lowered both hands to her body to pull her ass cheeks apart, pull her pussy lips wide and hold her open as, in one fluid motion, I used my grip on her to shove her down onto my cock.

3

nna

He lowered me, pushing me down hard and fast and exactly the way I wanted it. The size of his cock took me by surprise. I groaned as he stretched me, filled me like never before. I exhaled in a whoosh as Jack growled, a noise that struck me as oddly wild and territorial. We stood totally still as I shifted my hips, tried to accommodate his cock, which would have been much too big for me if I wasn't so turned on. If I wasn't so damn wet for him.

Why him?

Sure, he was big and gorgeous and way too complicated for a girl like me. But my body didn't give a shit about any of that. My brain melted down the first time he kissed me. But this longing, this want? This desperate need for him to fill me, kiss me? To move. God I needed him to *move.*

"God, Jack. Move. Fuck me." I bit down on his shoulder in silent demand. He'd woken months of suppressed lust, desire, need. I was starving for him, like an animal waking from a long hibernation. I needed him hard and fast and hot. He lifted a hand to my hair and pulled, angling my head up so I was forced to look into his eyes. The dominant move made my pussy clench around him and I whimpered, lost in him.

"You want me, princess? You need more?"

"Yes." God yes. Hurry the fuck up, yes.

My body is a traitor, I thought as I gave over to Jack's expert thrusts. His hands were no less punishing than his cock, which he used to hold my ass, to lift and lower me onto his thrusting length. I'd have marks there later, but for now, God, it was so good.

"I'm not taking it easy on you *this time,* princess. Hold on tight," he gritted out as I bit my lip and grabbed his shoulders, holding on because he was the only thing in my world. My entire existence narrowed to his scent, his heat, his hard, hot thrusts as he filled me to the point of pain. I held on so I wouldn't float away. I was out of control, spinning, fighting for air.

It took a few moments for his words to filter into

my lust fogged brain. *This time? There would only ever be this one time!* I barely had time to think it before he pulsed into me again and stole my train of thought.

"Bring it, Jack," I challenged as I dug my fingers into his shoulders harder. In response, he flexed those taut muscles and hips to push his dick in and out of me faster. The slide of his full length, the sharp zing of his cock hitting me deep inside, nudging my womb with each thrust, and the sheer width of him was enough to shut me up.

I let go and so did he. He watched me like I was the only thing that existed in his world. If I bit my lip, he saw me do it. If I moaned, her heard me. If I closed my eyes because I felt overwhelmed and needy and out of control, he always brought me back, demanded I look at him.

He wanted to own me, see me. I'd never felt like I did in that moment, like I was the only person in the world that mattered. Fires raged in his eyes, dominant and frustrated and possessive. Every conversation we'd had came rushing to the surface as he pinned me against the wall and I saw something between us I hadn't seen before.

Over the weeks and months, this tension had been building between us.

I held his gaze, unwilling to break, unwilling to look away as he fucked me, as his chocolate eyes blazed and his jaw locked .

Jack's dick pounded into me mercilessly and, for my part, I reveled in his wildness, in the rough and barely controlled nature of him. He was all man, rough and demanding and I melted instinctively, loved the way his dominant and possessive touch made me feel.

Wanted. Safe. Feminine. Powerful.

Beautiful.

There was no doubt I'd be sore tomorrow, but I didn't care. I had no idea I liked it so rough, but with Jack, it was... primitive. Hot. Perfect.

I nibbled and sucked his neck, his lips, his beautiful fucking jawline. I claimed him with my mouth while he claimed me with his cock. I relinquished my body to him, almost too shocked to believe this side of him was real, so raw and feral and demanding.

As if he read my thoughts, Jack chuckled darkly through his forced breaths. "Didn't expect this from a city boy, did you, princess?"

Each one of his words was punctuated by a thrust. I held his gaze for a split second before I closed them and moaned. I didn't care if he heard, if he knew what he did to me. I couldn't hide my responses from him. Not only could he see me, really see me, but he could feel it with my pussy walls rippling around him.

Jack's thrusts almost made me come right there, but I arched my back, rubbing my clit on the hard wall of his abdomen just right. He hooked my knees over his arms and spread me open wide, pushing me back into the wall so he could grind his body against me.

I was on the edge instantly, and his slight groans sank into my body and swirled in my head, pushing me over the edge. They were too sensual, too honest. He sounded like a man who barely held it together, and *fuck* that was hot. My nails scored his shoulders, his back, his neck, and pulled at his hair.

"More," I commanded.

His large, rough hands trailed to my nipples and he tugged them *hard* as I used the wall as a brace. Yes, that was the *more* I was looking for.

Everything hit critical mass and my back straightened against the wall involuntarily. The movement shoved Jack back, forcing him to hold me lower on my hips. I realized, a split second before it happened, that this new angle let Jack hit my G-spot, and he did. He rammed against that sensitive bundle of nerves as my moans and cries became unintelligible. My nails lashed out as I lost all capacity for thought. I scratched against his pecs, his biceps. I was lost in a spiral of orgasm that I couldn't stop.

Jack's own groan of pleasure warned me that my the rippling walls of my pussy and my incoherent cries pushed him to his own release. I tightened my inner muscles over and over, pulsing over him, pulling him deep so I could milk him to orgasm. As his forehead dropped to my sternum, his hands gripped the wall for strength. He fucked me faster, hitting my g-spot, rubbing my clit with his hard body and we came together in a flurry of cries and guttural exclamations. Jack's cock jerked so hard that it forced another yelp from me as my sensitive flesh reacted, my climax extended. He grazed gentle kisses down my chest, my raw nipples, the valley between my breasts as he filled me, coming more than I expected. I sighed a heavy, pleased sigh, one that told Jack just how satisfied I was. I would've been mad at myself for the display, except he let one out, too.

I smiled to myself and wrapped my arms around his neck to bring my mouth to his ear. "Well, that was surprising."

He chuckled as his hands gripped my hips for a final time. He lifted me off his cock, but my sex protested and clutched him tightly. We both moaned again as he continued to move me up and off his cock. I was left feeling empty and… still horny.

How the hell could I want more sex after that?

When he put me back on my feet, we just stared at each other. He'd stripped down, but I hadn't been given any time to stare. And boy, was he stare worthy. Muscle rippled from his wide chest to trim hips. His thighs were thick and strong. I wanted to rub my body all over him like a purring cat, but I leaned against the cool wall and held myself still. I'd felt those masculine muscles, such a contrast to my feminine curves. His body held so many contradictions to mine and all of them turned me on. Where I thought Jack would be soft, weak, he was strong, in control. He had shown me a side of him that I didn't expect, but wanted to see more of. I broke out of my reverie when I realized Jack stared at me, as well. His eyes caressed the skin of my face, my breasts, my stomach, my hips… my sex. I felt it clench again and stared at his hard cock, still covered with the very full condom. As if reading my mind, he removed it and tossed it into a small trash can under his coffee table.

I'd fucked him and we hadn't even made it out of the living room.

Did that make me a genius or a slut?

Looking at his rock hard body, I voted genius and told the guilt riddled good-little-girl to shut the hell up. Good girls didn't get to have this much fun. *Good girls* didn't get to fuck Jack Buchanan.

Jack cleared his throat and his dark brown eyes met mine. These weren't the angry eyes I was used to. Now I saw intensity, need, desire and it was all focused on me. My knees almost buckled at the sight. He began to slowly pad around me, one arm stroked my skin as he went. When he got to my backside, his hand came down swiftly on my ass. I heard a grunt of appreciation and knew he liked what he saw.

"That's for scaring the shit out of me."

Next, his finger slid down between my thighs and

through the wetness that still coated me there. "Next time won't be so quick," he whispered in my ear and the shivers he sent down my spine tickled the whole way. "I'm going to learn every curve of your gorgeous fucking body and I'm going to make you come even harder. Once wasn't enough. Then, after I'm done memorizing you from head-to-toe, I'm going to have a little fun."

For once in my life, I was stunned silent. Stone cold quiet. My mouth just gaped open and occasionally my teeth clacked together in an attempt to form sentences. Jack chuckled, a light and airy sound, as he gently took my hands and led me into his bedroom. I barely had brain power to register the dark paneling, the plush chaise lounge and the massive picture window. I was too stunned to speak, let alone think, as he kissed me gently.

Gently? I could handle rough and wild, but Jack being gentle? I didn't know what to think and I had no will to resist.

He pushed me down onto the soft plaid comforter with the storm's gray skies giving me the only light to watch as he paced next to the bed like a wild animal stalking prey.

Holy crap, he was ripped. And that cock? That had fit in me? Placing one knee on the bed and leaning over me, he trailed kisses from my lips, to my chin, to my throat. His hands roamed across my stomach, my arms, my thighs and his exploration lit me up. All my nerve endings had woken with our furious lovemaking in the living room and now they were standing at attention, happy to receive the attention from his mouth, his hands.

"Hmm," Jack pondered. "Where should I start?" he whispered as he nibbled the curve of my hip. His kisses trailed inwards, towards my core, and I gasped as his tongue licked at my folds.

"Mmm," he groaned against my sensitive flesh. "I think this is as good a place as any," he teased, and then our eyes met over the expanse of my belly. He flashed an insanely wicked smile before his face dove down and my head fell back into the pillows, conscious thought overruled by the feel of his tongue and fingers as he made me come again and again.

4

nna

I JERKED AWAKE. Realization dawned on me before my eyes fully opened.

I slept with Jack Buchanan! I'm a fucking idiot!

I sat up and the sheets slipped down, my bare flesh exposed. My nipples were hard, raw. And I felt... ridden. Swollen. Sore and still a little horny. *Thoroughly fucked*, as Jack called it last night.

I had to leave. I had to get the hell out of Jack's bed. I had to get the hell out of Alaska. Last night with Jack was a one-time thing, a mistake. I needed to bail before the ship took off on a course I didn't plan for. The orgasms he'd given me? Yeah, I could get addicted to them. The man himself was pretty damn addicting. He wasn't a jackass. He was just Jack, the hot guy who was wild and also tender in bed. Attentive. Inventive. Who made sure I came first... every time. I had no idea there were so many different positions—and surfaces—and ways to have sex.

He was on his back, one arm thrown over his head. Asleep, he wasn't as dangerous to me, but when he woke, when those dark eyes opened, they'd hold me captive.

Shit.

I looked for my clothes by the bed, but they were nowhere in sight. Carefully, I climbed from the bed. No way was I waking him. The weather had passed sometime during the night and the dawn was clear. Birds sang outside his home and light filtered through his thin, gauze like curtains. I had to be on that plane, leaving Jack and his bionic dick behind.

If Jack was a superhero, sex would be his superpower. And I had no chance of winning that war. My body craved him, even now. Worse, my heart ached when I stared at the five-o'clock shadow on his face, remembered the way his eyes had held my gaze, whispered such dark, erotic promises. Jack liked to talk, to tell me every naughty little thing he was going to do to my body.

Anticipation was almost worse than the cure. He had me so worked up last night, he'd barely had to breathe over my clit and I'd come apart at the seams, screaming his name like a wild woman.

Yes. My only recourse, if I wanted to save my sanity, was to run away like a coward.

I peeked around the open bedroom door, spied his shirt on the floor in the living room, and tiptoed toward it. My shirt was a few feet away, rumpled and still damp and missing every single button. I slid Jack's shirt around my shoulders and buttoned it up. I picked up my wet socks, pulled up my chafing, wet jeans, and slipped on my boots. They were all disgustingly wet, but I only needed to get back home. I braced myself for Jack's voice or footsteps from the bedroom, but heard nothing. I snuck to the door, turned the knob, and silently prayed that he wouldn't hear.

As I slipped around the south end of the house and headed for the tree line, I felt a slight tug in my chest, guilt over my grand escape.

He doesn't deserve to wake up alone in that king sized bed. He was so great last night.

Thoughts swirled back into my mind and I remembered the feel of Jack's hot breath on the nape of my neck as he took me again, this time from behind. He was true to his word; he had worked every inch of my body before he finally gave me his cock, which I had begged for in the end. His masculine, rough hands took me by the hips as his cock pounded into me, my nerves frayed as I came again. And again. I lost count at some point, something I've never done with other men since it wasn't all that hard to count to zero, or occasionally one.

I continued to stalk down the path through the trees, headed for the water, but my mind was back in the cabin. Suddenly, I recalled Jack's rough stubble against my hip. My breath stuttered and my foot slipped on a tree stump as I remembered his nibble on the soft skin of my inner thigh. At some point, he'd whispered, "I'm going to take good care of you, baby. This time, it's all about you," as his mouth settled over my pussy. He had braced me against him as I bucked with my orgasm, totally out of control. I let out a little groan of appreciation, my knees weak from the sheer amount of pleasure he had given me.

My core clenched at the thought of Jack's mouth on me.

See, this was exactly why I had to get the hell out, I scolded myself and picked up the pace.

I kept one eye on the house as I moved and hoped Jack wouldn't open the door and see my bright plaid in the trees. Finally far enough away from the cabin, I snuck onto the dock, my eyes peeled for signs of movement from behind me. Sighing with relief, I turned in the direction of my plane and ran smack-dab into Jack Fucking Buchanan.

"Where do you think you're going, Ms. Jackson?" he asked. His face could have been carved from stone and I had no idea if he was angry, hurt, or just being a dick.

I bounced off his chest, straightened, and glared at him to cover for my flushed face. He wore low-slung jeans and nothing else, which meant his Grecian skin glowed in the Alaskan sun. I felt like a slob in comparison, shoved into still-damp clothes and squishy boots. This was the worst walk of shame. Ever.

"Where did you come from?" I spit out. *Brilliant comeback, Anna.* I stepped around him to peer at my plane. I forgot about Jack for a moment as the full extent of the storm's wrath became clear in the morning sun. The right floater was badly dented, so bad that my poor baby lilted to the side, barely staying afloat. *Shit.* There was no way in hell I could take off or land on the water with the floater looking like that. Jack cleared his throat and I resumed glaring at him.

"My bed, which is where you were until five minutes ago." He stared at me, daring me to say... what? "Which is where you should be right now."

"I can't stay here, Jack." I didn't have the time or patience to explain things to him. He was too dangerous. He was like my personal kryptonite and if I stayed here with him, if he asked, I would *stay*. In Alaska. Here. Living in nowhere.

"Well, you aren't going anywhere right now. It appears you nearly tore off one of your floaters when you ass-planted the plane last night," he said when he turned to look at my plane. "Wonder what else you shook loose."

My heart sped up a bit at the thought of my close call last night. I knew I was lucky, that it could have been much worse, but it also embarrassed the hell out of me when I remembered that Jack had watched me 'ass-plant' the plane, as he put it. That only made me angry and defensive. I'd survived. Every landing was a good landing, right?

"Could you land a floatplane in a massive storm? Or fly a plane at all, City Boy? No? Didn't think so," I snapped and bit down my desire to kick him in the crotch, but then I remembered what he'd been able to do with that crotch.

I pushed him out of the way to inspect the damage further and groaned.

Jack peered curiously around me to look at the floater. "I'm not a pilot, but that looks a little messed up." He said it innocently enough but it picked at my last thread.

"You *think*, Jack? No, I can't fly, or land a floatplane without my floats! I have to call in another pilot to deliver the part. I'm stuck here until then."

"I can think of some things we can do to pass the time."

I couldn't help but notice that the low cut of his jeans gave me a sneak peek of the curve of his ass, the dimples on his lower back. The scratches up and down his golden skin. *Marks I put there.*

"And you look good enough to eat wearing my shirt."

Sex. On. A Stick. He was deadly. Irresistible. And I was wearing his shirt, the warmth and scent of him teasing my senses in the slight morning breeze.

"No." I shook my head. "No, no, no. *No.* This was supposed to be one night. That's it."

He shrugged, the corner of his mouth tipping up. "I can drive you into town to see if the mercantile has a spare. Chances are pretty good. Or you can call it in. Either way, this—" He waved his hand between us. "—is more than just one night, princess. Just ask your pussy. She knows."

I nearly burst out laughing, but the urge was barely conquered by outrage. I didn't know what he meant by the *more than one night* comment and I stood there, shocked into silence as I watched him walk down the dock and up the path into the woods.

I followed, knowing standing on the dock was a complete waste of time. One night. One. Then why did my nipples tighten at the idea of one more? I tried to forget the feel of his whiskers against my breast last night. Or the way he stilled when he came for the third time, his jaw clenched and eyes closed tightly. How he had made me laugh when he flipped me over to sit on top of him, cowgirl style. Or the way we had smiled at each other afterwards and fell asleep in each other's arms.

Nope. Definitely not thinking about any of that.

5

ack

THE DRIVE into town was tense, to say the least. I wanted to spank Anna's ass for trying to sneak away. *What the fuck was that all about? We had a great night together and she wanted to leave without even a goodbye?*

As I gripped the steering wheel, my thoughts trailed back to the night before, to my three massive, mind-blowing orgasms. I lost count with hers, and I didn't even try to suppress the primitive and very macho sense of satisfaction that filled me knowing I'd worked her body like a master, made her come over and over until she was putty in my hands, until she gave me everything. She fit me perfectly. We were *good* together and that surprised the shit out of me.

Sure, the tension between us for the past months hadn't been anger, but simmering chemistry, which decided to boil over last night. There was definitely something between us, something more than just sex.

But she tried to leave you, asshole.

Clothes dry, there was nothing I could do about her shirt. And I didn't really want to. I loved the fact that she was wearing mine.

I had tried to keep myself busy making coffee and breakfast earlier that morning, but nothing helped. She was like a magnet and I couldn't stop wanting her. Even now I knew her panties were in the dryer and she wore no bra and I could see out of the corner of my eye her breasts sway with every rut and bump of the damn dirt road on our way in to town.

Did she have any idea the affect she had on me?

A few minutes into the drive, Anna leaned back in her bucket seat and took a deep breath. "I'm sorry I tried to leave this morning without saying goodbye. It's just... complicated. I don't want a relationship, I don't need anything mucking up my chances of getting out of Alaska. Don't take it personal," she added with a short glance in my direction. I perked up at the comment. *Getting out of Alaska.*

"Where are you going if you leave Alaska? Don't you have family here?" I asked, eyes focused on the bumpy, pothole-covered dirt road.

"No, my dad died last year," Anna mumbled sadly. "I figured you knew since he'd been the one to make deliveries before me. I have no reason to stay up here, aside from our house. I've tried to sell it, but no takers yet. Once that sells, I'm out of here," she told me, her gaze on her intertwined fingers in her lap.

"I didn't hear about your father. I'm sorry," I said and let the quiet fall over us for a second.

"Thanks," she whispered and we both settled into a comfortable silence for the rest of the drive. My brain didn't shut off, though, as I thought about this fiery, beautiful woman who wanted to leave Alaska. Who wanted to leave me and run headlong into the chaos and noise I'd been running from for the past year.

Alaska, my middle of nowhere cabin, had become home for me. But as I tried, unsuccessfully, to ignore the passionate woman sitting next to me, I wondered how long that would remain true if she left Alaska, and me, behind.

When we arrived at the mercantile, Anna stomped inside excitedly, my clothes on her all rolled up and oddly adorable. *She's so low-maintenance,* I marveled as I walked in behind her. My thoughts flew back to Victoria, to the manicures and constant hair styling. To the thousand dollar purses, to the nursery bedding. To the baby.

Nope! Not going there, Buchanan. Focus.

I shook off the memory and the sting that came with it and looked around the store.

I grabbed a basket by the front door and worked my way down the first shelf. I grabbed a few things I knew I needed, that I didn't need to pay Anna to fly in. Peanut butter, toilet paper, magazines, the usual. I didn't know how fucking boring Alaska was until I'd lived here for a few months. Now, I never underestimated the value of a good magazine.

I heard Anna's voice at the back counter, clear as a bell. She talked in a gentle, familiar way, like she knew the person. As I approached, I heard her ask the clerk about his arthritis. The older man asked questions about her in turn, and they gossiped for a bit over other townies.

By the time I got back to the counter, I'd added only one other item to my basket and I smiled in anticipation of Anna's reaction. She turned and watched me approach, and her eyes trailed from my boots to my forearms, exposed by my rolled-up sleeves. They lingered in all the right places and I grinned when her gaze finally reached mine just to make sure she knew that I'd noticed.

"Well? Any luck?" I asked as I leaned against the counter. The clerk smiled kindly at me, an old man with fisherman's skin, rough and weathered. "Sorry, sir, but we don't have the floater she needs for her craft. It'll have to be flown in from Anchorage, and that'll be a few days."

Anna groaned, clearly unhappy about this turn of events. I bit my lip to keep from smiling, but failed miserably.

"It would appear we are stuck together for the week, Ms. Jackson. Is there anything you want to pick up? I've got a few staples, but feel free to add to the basket." Right on cue, Anna peeked into the basket, where her eyes fell on the large box of condoms I had placed right on top. She rolled her eyes and made a very unladylike noise in the back of her throat. I chuckled as she stomped off down the food aisles and I unloaded my loot on the counter.

As we piled the bags of basic goods into the back of my truck, I heard Anna's stomach growl. I chastised myself as I realized she hadn't eaten much. I'd cooked breakfast, but she'd barely nibbled on a piece of toast. She hadn't complained, but I knew that wasn't her way. She was a challenge, an enigma I would be forced to unravel until she trusted me to take care of her.

I wanted that trust. I wanted her to feel safe enough to complain, to rant and rail and cry, but knew I'd have to earn that place in her life. Victoria had handed me everything on a silver platter, made me believe she loved me. But I was smarter than that now, and I knew a woman's heart had to be earned.

Hunger bubbled up in my own stomach as I turned to her.

"We should go run by the cafe real quick, get some food before we head back."

She nodded and we walked, shoulder-to-shoulder, to the only thing that resembled a restaurant in this podunk little town. They only served a few things and all were excellent. I just learned the first time I came not to ask what kind of meat was in the pot roast. It never was beef. Sometimes it was moose, sometimes caribou. When we entered, everyone turned to stare and when they saw Anna, a handful came over to ask her how she was. Not me. Her.

Anna answered their questions gracefully, with

jokes and gentle ribbings all around. I felt a slight tug in my chest as I watched her around these people who obviously cared for her. And she obviously cared for them.

So why is she leaving?

She asked after everyone's spouses, kids, grandkids, random aches and pains. The entire small cafe talked as we sat in our booth and I, once again, felt a slight pang at the sense of community, of friendship. I'd been here before, but I'd been the outsider and hadn't received this kind of reception. Still was. It had been a long time since I had been around people, much less a group that actually gave a damn about each other. I missed it and that surprised the hell out of me.

I'd spent years in corporate boardrooms, building my teams, tackling a seemingly impossible task together. I loved that aspect of building something from nothing. And I'd let one woman, a woman—I realized now—I barely knew, wreck me and make me doubt myself in a fundamental way.

With Anna, I never stopped to think long enough to doubt myself. She made me uninhibited, spontaneous and a little out of control. She made me feel alive and challenged me in a way Victoria never had.

I lost myself in thought while Anna told one of the older ladies that she would help the woman move some of her furniture around when Anna stopped by with deliveries next time. Then an old guy across the cafe started talking to his friends about how everyone had helped another resident raise a roof the weekend before. So few people lived in this town and yet they helped each other any way they could.

Was this how it was, back in Seattle? Had I simply forgotten?

The fog covering my emotions lifted as if the need to isolate myself became less as I sat next to this woman and her neighbors. A little bit of the drive that I feared Victoria had crushed out of me sputtered back to life as I soaked in the friendly, supportive atmosphere, the tightly knit group of people had all known each other for years.

Anna turned away from her friends, her fellow townies, and refocused her attention on me. My breath stilled a bit at the sight of her green eyes as they glanced toward me. She smiled briefly and ordered for both of us when the waitress came.

"What?" she asked when I kept staring at her. "You don't like caribou hot dogs?"

I gave a slight shoulder shrug. "Never had them."

She grinned and pulled a course, white napkin from the dispenser that rested on the table next to the salt and pepper shakers. "You'll love 'em. My favorite."

In my previous life, that would've never happened, a woman ordering for me. In this life, I began to see that there was no way around Anna's impetuous behavior. She was completely unpredictable, and I loved it. She made me feel alive. Which brought me full circle.

"Why are you leaving Alaska? Won't you miss it?" I wondered. Perhaps asking her in a diner full of friends wasn't the best place, but I wanted to know. Why would she leave behind everyone she knew and loved?

I knew why I had left Seattle, but Anna? She was different. She belonged. These people weren't just acquaintances or employees, they were friends and neighbors. Family. They cared about her.

She took a moment and collected herself, waiting to respond until after the waitress dropped off our drinks.

"My mom died when I was four, a snowmobiling accident if you *must* know. I don't really remember her, but Dad was crazy about her. He and I flew deliveries and packages all over after she died. He taught me how to fly and that plane on your dock was his. He died a year ago, like I said. Died in his sleep. Doc said it was a heart attack."

She took a moment and paused, clearly upset at the memory. I considered jumping in to apologize but she took off again.

"After Dad died, I just started thinking, 'What's the point?' You know? What's the point of me being here, doing this, when I don't have any reason to stay? I could finally get out of here. Go see the world. Travel. Start a new charter business somewhere new. I could do a lot," she finished, her eyes misty. "I've been taking business and management classes online to finish my bachelor's degree. I'm hoping that, when I do finally leave, I can start my own charter business flying tourists around. Maybe even manage a small airport. But without the money from selling Dad's house, I can't leave yet. Soon, though," Anna added quietly. She almost smiled, but then seemed to remember that this little show-n-tell session was all thanks to me asking.

I was stunned. I hadn't realized she was so eager to leave, that so much thought had gone into her master plan. College. Selling her home. Those were big risks for someone with no support system, no family to fall back on. I just assumed she was a twenty-four-year-old girl who dreamed of Big City lights. And here I was, wrong, and quiet as a damn tree stump. I shook my head and cleared the thoughts. I coughed before I finally found my voice; I felt like the World's Biggest Dick.

"Anna, I'm sorry. I had no idea it was like that. Please forgive me for being such an ass," I leaned forward and stroked her hand. She jerked it back and I felt a little rubber band snap in my chest, a physical sting from her rejection.

"Yeah, well, what's *your* story, Jack? How did a city

boy like you end up in nowhere, Alaska hiding from the world?"

Anna's eyes were lit with curiosity, and I started talking before I could sensor the words. I took a deep breath and decided to tell her everything. I hadn't cared what people thought before, but now, I wanted Anna to know the truth. Needed her to understand.

"Well, just over a year ago I sold my latest startup and moved up here from Seattle. Made a pretty penny on it but lost most of it on my ex. She told me she was having my baby… but she lied." I paused and took a deep breath.

I looked at Anna quickly to see if she was smirking because I'd been so stupid to let Victoria take advantage of me, but instead I saw the same regret on her face that I had felt when she told me her story. She wasn't judging me, not yet.

"Her name was Victoria. We were dating, she got pregnant, and I always wanted to be a father, so…"

"You married her."

"Stupid, right?" I ran my hands through my hair and plowed ahead with the gory details. "We'd been married almost a year when her ex showed up one day, demanding a paternity test and a hundred grand."

"Oh, God."

I grinned, but knew the humor didn't reach my eyes. "Well, I don't know if God had anything to do with it, but the test came back and I wasn't daddy anymore. I lost my baby girl and my wife in one day to some asshole investment broker I'd introduced her to at a corporate party."

"Jeez, Jack. She was a bitch. I'm so sorry."

"The worse of it was, I sold my startup so I could be with her and the baby, bought all the baby stuff, even bought a 'Dad car' to hold the car seat. I loved that little girl. Jack Buchanan, the big billionaire businessman dropped everything for a baby. Her mother was difficult and, to be honest, I didn't love her like I should have. But I did the right thing. And then I found out… she was sleeping around on me and the baby wasn't actually mine." My breath stuttered in my chest and I took a big gulp of my soda to hide my moment of weakness.

Anna's small hands reached across the green laminate table and she gripped mine fiercely. "Jack, I'm so, so sorry. I had no idea, *I'm* the asshole for always being such a bitch to you. I can't believe you never told me, even when I teased you all the time…" her eyes misted over again and I reached over to stroke her cheek.

"It's okay, really. You deserve to know and it's time I told someone. I sold my business and came to the cabin for a quick vacation. Didn't leave. I just fell in love with Alaska, and I haven't been home since. I keep lying to myself, and everyone else for that matter. I told my family I stay up here because I'm not ready to go work with my cousins, that Alaska is just too relaxing.

But that's a lie. I'm just not ready to face my memories back in Seattle."

The words left my mouth and I felt a huge rush of relief as the truth finally came out. My mother was the only one who knew and I was pretty sure that was why she hired Anna to bring my groceries. Had she been playing matchmaker?

Well, she's going to be pissed when she finds out the woman of my dreams is leaving Alaska.

Yeah, this woman, this feisty, tiny little spitfire of a woman was the one I wanted.

We sat in companionable silence before Anna sat up a bit straighter, uncomfortable again.

"Jack... why didn't you ever make a move before? All those times I delivered to you, I knew you were interested. At least in my tits and ass," she added with a chuckle. "Men are forward up here. But you never did anything. That's why I assumed you were neutered," she laughed, but only to cover the insecurity I saw in her eyes.

"You don't need anyone, Anna. I could tell. You are gorgeous, drop dead gorgeous," I added as I looked directly into her fiery gaze. "You don't need anyone to help you fly a plane, unload heavy coolers, chop wood... anything. You're wholly yourself. And I mistook that for disinterest, so I didn't make a move," I finished as I leaned forward in the well-worn booth. "If

I'd known how hot you'd burn, I would have dragged you to bed the first time I saw you."

She blushed furiously and refused to meet my eyes. She fiddled with her silverware and she bit her lip, all while she kept her head down. "I have to be able to do all that because I'm on my own now. Do I want to do it all? Yes, but just so that I know I can. Do I want to do it all by myself forever?" She shook her head. "No, I don't."

What was she saying? She wanted someone to take care of her? She wanted *me* to take care of her?

"What made you...change your mind last night?" she asked timidly, which shocked me. *Anna? Timid?*

"I thought you were going to die, crash your plane into the ice cold lake. I don't know what happened, Anna, you just woke me up. I've been asleep at the wheel for a while now, and something about you made me change." She lifted her gaze and her eyes were soft and round. This conversation was getting way to heavy for caribou hot dogs. "Besides, I realized that I'd be rather upset if you died before I got to see the perfect tits you're always trying to hide beneath those long-sleeved shirts."

Anna gasped, pulled her straw from her drink, and threw it directly in my face. She giggled mercilessly as I leapt from my side of the booth and dragged her out of her own. She stopped giggling and softened against me.

"Well, Mr. Buchanan," Anna's sultry voice echoed in my ear. "I do believe we have a few days until my parts come in. We might as well go back to your place make the most of it."

"Let's get those caribou dogs to go."

I barely remembered the drive home. All I could think about was *making the most of it.*

6

nna

When we got back to the cabin, we barely made it inside before our clothes were ripped off and our lips locked in pure lust. For two days straight, Jack and I took full advantage of my circumstances. If there was some other part of the cabin to have sex in, Jack didn't know about it. He fucked me against the cold wood-paneled walls, against the shiny oak floors, bent over his sleek granite counters in the kitchen. At one point on the second day, we attempted to crawl to the bedroom, but made it only to the plush rug in the hallway. We even did it in various positions I didn't recall in the Kama Sutra. Bent over the chaise lounge in his master bedroom, laid across the beautiful stone bench in the shower, straddled on top of him on the desk in his study, on the swing that overlooked the water. I was worn ragged but always starved for more.

The entire time, I was in a state of constant ecstasy, one orgasm spilled into the next. We stopped only for food, and even *that* became it's own kind of fun.

Jack whispered in my ear throughout our sex marathon and he worshipped me with his hands. He told me I was beautiful, that I drove him crazy. He paid attention to my body in ways that I hadn't known existed, and he claimed parts of me no one else had. His attentions and affections told me he felt it, too. Whatever *it* was, it made both of us crazed for each other. I felt like an addict. I couldn't get enough, and as soon as he was done with me, I wanted more.

We had a connection. I felt it each time our lips met, as yet another orgasm slammed into me.

By the end of the second day, we took it slow, the edge finally worn off. Jack's hands reached for my ass as he moved his dick in and out, in and out, just as another orgasm rippled down my spine. He held my legs spread apart while I splayed across the sheets and he dripped sweat down his glorious, tan chest. He was worn down, too, but neither of us stopped. Neither of us wanted to.

His jaw was tense and all of his muscles strained as he held back his orgasm… for me. "I'm going to make you come two more times, princess, then it's my turn," he bit out, barely audible over the moans of ecstasy I shed.

That totally worked for me.

Jack placed the pad of his thumb on my clit and, immediately soaked with my desire, rubbed circles around the already-sensitive bundle. As if my body couldn't handle more, my back arched and Jack's mouth settled over my breasts. He licked my nipples and bit down just as he smacked my clit roughly. The shockwaves went from my sex to my nipples and back down again as the orgasm came from somewhere in my core.

Jack's assailing thumb and mouth didn't stop, though, and the tension from the last orgasm barely subsided before it turned into yet another one. As the friction from his cock and hand became unbearable, he whispered, "Scream for me, baby."

And I did.

I woke up sometime later, alone. I was still dazed from my orgasms and the sound Jack made as he finally came. It was territorial, guttural, and somehow vulnerable. Like I undid him.

Oh no, you don't, my rational brain shouted at me. *Now is not the time to fall for someone. Now is the time to leave Alaska, remember?* I didn't bother to tell my rational self I already fell for him; I knew it.

I stood up and found one of Jack's shirts on the floor, slipped it on. As I did up the buttons, I worried that my body already knew what my head did not.

I'm in too deep.

My dreams were too important, too big, to be derailed by a guy who wanted to hide away in the Alaska wilderness. No matter how much Jack meant to me, I was leaving Alaska. It was that simple and that difficult all at once.

I peeked into the living room and wondered where Jack was. I heard a small noise from the study, nestled down another hall. Jack sat leisurely at his computer, sweatpants hung low on his waist and no shirt to be seen.

Probably because I ripped it.

He hadn't seen me from the angle he faced his computer screen from, so I stealthily tiptoed around to his back, prepared to scare the daylights out of him.

"You're incredibly un-sneaky, princess," Jack declared as he spun his chair to face me. Apparently, "Sneaky" was not my middle name. Jack pulled me to him, situated me on his lap, and spun the chair back to his computer. He buried his face in my hair and breathed deeply.

"You smell like me. I like that," he whispered in my ear.

I pretended to not like his words and instead glanced at his computer screen.

What did the serious Mr. Buchanan look at while I was sleeping? Porn?

"What's this?" I asked him and reached for the mouse. I straightened as I recognized the logo of a company based out of Seattle: Buchanan Technology. "Family business?"

"My cousins. It's a startup of theirs. It's doing well and they want me to come work for them," Jack mused as he reached to close out of the window.

"A *startup*?" I chuckled, because the company looked a little more in the red than just a startup. "Are you going to do it? Invest in them? Get back on the horse?"

He must have read my mind because he said, "It's not much of a startup at this point, not when they're bringing in millions a year. They want me to help them push it to billions."

Billions. Jeez.

I looked at his bare chest and dragged my thoughts back to the conversation with difficulty. Our eyes met and he smirked knowingly, but said, "They're family. Plus, a solid portfolio, tons of success thus far, a steady team, a great business model... They have all the right parts." He punctuated this last statement when he stroked my "right part," which jerked me upright. "My cousins can wait. There are other projects I'm involved in that are keeping my attention at the moment."

Jack leaned in to kiss me as he reached up beneath my shirt to cup my breast gently. My nails slid down his arms to his elbows, then to the waist of his sweatpants.

"Yes, Mr. Buchanan." I nodded against his lips. "I think I'd like to explore this opportunity myself."

I giggled as he lifted me off his lap, placed me on his hard desk. Nudging my knees wide, he settled himself between them. When his fingers coasted up my inner thighs, I fell back.

"When I give a project my attention—" His lips followed the same path until his hot breath fanned over my pussy. "I give it *all* my attention."

I AWOKE to the sound of a prop plane engine just overhead and then I heard the unmistakable sound of floats as they cut through the water.

The plane! My replacement float is here.

I sat up bolt upright but forgot that Jack laid next to me on the floor of his study. We'd settled there after revisiting his desk.

I smacked him in the face in my rush to peek out the window and he groaned, rolling over. "What the hell, Princess?"

I ignored him and made it to the window just in time; the pilot had turned toward the dock and I heard the lack of noise that indicated his engine was turned off.

"My float is here. I need to go out and meet the pilot!"

I sprinted towards my clothes, finding one of the shirts I'd borrowed by the fireplace, my pants in the kitchen. Spinning about, naked, I looked for my panties.

"Looking for these?" Jack stood there, my panties dangling from his finger.

Grabbing them from him, I threw everything on haphazardly, and ran to the door. The pilot, Joe, was on the dock, tugging his anchor loose. He was an old friend of my dad's and I was happy to see him. We talked about the damage to my float, the storm I nearly crash landed in, and Dad's place.

"I heard someone put in an offer?" Joe asked and my heart stilled.

"What? Really? I haven't heard anything, I've been here for almost three days, no contact," I stuttered out.

Sold? The house sold?

"Well, from the sounds of it, you got yourself a deal. You moving to Seattle with the money?" Joe asked as he pulled my spare float from his cargo hold.

I tried, and failed, to ignore the stinging image of Jack that came to mind when I said, "Yep, ready to rock as soon as the papers are signed."

Joe and I worked diligently for the next hour as we turned my plane to face the dry shore. We pulled the dented float off and screwed the new one on, a feat that would have been unmanageable if Jack hadn't come out to help.

"Not bad for a City Boy," I nudged Jack as we scrubbed our hands in the freezing cold water to clean the grease off. Joe was nice enough to go through the safety checks on my plane before he climbed into his own, cleared the signals, and started his propellers. He waved as he turned towards the open water, ready to take off. Jack and I watched his plane grow smaller and smaller before we spoke, the unwanted words hanging in the air between us.

Time to bite the bullet, Anna. I took a deep breath. "Jack, I—," I managed to start.

He cut in. "Don't leave yet, princess."

Jack's brown eyes were full of pain and unspoken emotion and it nearly undid me. But I pulled it together and clasped his hands.

As I looked into his eyes, I said, "It's been really,

really great. These were probably the best few days of my life. It's definitely been the best sex." I laughed, but Jack didn't find it funny. "But you and I both know *this* —whatever *this* is—wouldn't extend past that. I need someone who wants to live life to the fullest, go out into the world and go on adventures with me, not someone who wants to hide out here."

Those last words came out as a blow, I knew it, but I needed them to sting enough for him to let me go. For me to push him away enough so I could get on the plane.

Jack's eyes turned cold; clearly the comment hit him like I'd intended. I felt a punch somewhere in my solar plexus at the sight, at the realization that I hurt him. But I took my chance and backed away from him slowly. I had nothing to load up; everything was still in the cockpit. I had my clothes, I had my new float. *Time to rock and roll.*

Just as I stepped onto the foothold, I made the mistake of looking back. Jack stood there on the dock, pants soaked to the thighs and white T-shirt streaked with grease from the float bolts. His brown, wavy hair was tossed in the wind and mussed from my fingers running through it again and again; I couldn't help but smile. I leapt down from the foothold and walked slowly to him, prepared to give him one last kiss.

"Anna, don't go," he pleaded as he took my face in

his hands. I angled myself up on tiptoes to kiss him softly on his bowed, perfect lips. "I love you."

I hugged him and, as I did, whispered, "I love you too, Jack." And I did, but I couldn't stay.

He looked down at me, confused. "I'll see you next week, right? My regular delivery?" he asked and attempted a wink. I smiled noncommittally and backed away, soaking in the last sight of him. I wasn't coming back. I couldn't.

I turned and jogged back to the cockpit, stepped all the way up, and kick started the propellers. The anchor dragged up too slowly for my liking and I watched Jack pace the length of the dock like a caged tiger. His tan skin gleamed and his chocolate eyes looked a little misty, but just as I almost lost sight of the dock, I saw his arm wave in goodbye. A single motion but my heart broke at the gesture.

Goodbye, Jack.

I cleared the water and flew north, away from the cabin, away from Jack, away from my life in Alaska, tears streaming down my face as I left behind the only man I'd ever loved.

7

ack

THE WEEK PASSED SO FUCKING slow as I waited to hear Anna's old floatplane fly overhead. Sometimes, I thought I heard the propellers of her plane from the north and I ran towards the front door, out onto the lawn, and peered straight up. Each time, I was embarrassed at the level of disappointment I felt in the hollow of my chest.

I was totally whipped. I knew I'd see her again in just a few days, but my pillow smelled like her, my study smelled like her, and I couldn't get her out of my head. Hell, we'd fucked on practically every horizontal surface in my house. There was literally nowhere in my house I could look without seeing her, hearing her, feeling her.

Missing her.

I tried to shake off the Anna-induced fog and made one big move, one that would set my course for the foreseeable future. I sent an email to connect with Seth and Ben. We scheduled a conference call, outlined my involvement in the company, and were ready to bring me back into the Buchanan fold. They were welcoming me on board as a consultant. I was back in the game and it felt good. Most of all, though, I couldn't wait to share the news with Anna. This meant that we could leave Alaska... *together*. That our paths would be parallel rather than star-crossed.

The day came, finally, for Anna to deliver my groceries. I sat around the living room, unable to even consider work or research. As the afternoon approached, I became downright agitated. I paced like a madman around my house.

Where the fuck was she?

There was no storm, no reason to delay. I nearly worked myself into a frenzy when I heard it—the faintest sound of a prop engine plane coming from the north. I stood stock-still, just to be sure it was actually a plane before I ran into the yard like a maniac. *Again.*

The noise grew louder and I leapt for the door; I nearly pulled it off the hinges in my excitement. I launched off the patio and hustled across the lawn, my eyes on the sky. I saw it— Anna's plane—as she swooped over the treeline, coasted a few dozen feet off the water, and then landed with grace just to the south. She steered the plane to the dock, cut the engine, and anchored just as her floatplane drifted with a gentle bump into my dock. I had already made it to the dock and covered the twenty or so feet to her cockpit in just a few bounds. I yanked the door open and was greeted by...

"Joe?" I asked, my entire worldview tilted and tipped on its ass. The old man looked just as shocked as I did. Probably because I yanked his cockpit door open with more eagerness than he was used to when making deliveries.

"Yes, Mr. Buchanan," Joe answered. "You had a delivery set for today? Sorry if I'm late, I had to fuel up before I flew out here. Long trip home."

Joe smiled weakly.

"I have all your goods in the cargo hold, if you'll just let me..."

He shifted out of the cockpit but couldn't move with me in his space. I shook myself and moved back, still too stunned to speak. He stepped onto the dock, opened the cargo hold, and pulled out the two coolers full of my damn groceries.

As he did so, Joe added, "Guess you heard about Anna by now. Finally sold her daddy's house. The offer came in when she was stuck here with you, actually. Buyer bought it with cash the day she got back home. She was so excited. She took the first flight out to Seattle as soon as she was packed."

The old man struggled to push the heavy coolers to the dock and my senses kicked in long enough to help him. We carried the coolers into the cabin and Joe, nice as he was, helped me unload. The entire time, my mind whirred with noise.

She wasn't coming. She left. Gone.

I looked out the window at the plane and I turned to face Joe. "You have her floatplane," I stated dumbly.

Joe looked up from the cooler with a slightly bemused look on his face and answered, "Yeah, she sold it to me. Tried to give it to me, but it's a good old girl. I paid her a fair price. She's gonna need the money to get settled down south. And I helped her daddy keep it up all those years, I guess she wanted me to have it."

That was it; the final blow. She sold her plane, her only way she had to make a living up here. That meant she was done. She was gone, *really* gone. I thumped down on the barstool in the kitchen and stared at my hands as that realization sank in.

To avoid being a total pussy, I cleared my throat and asked Joe the last question I could think of, "Do you know where she is? Did she leave a number to call…just in case?"

I had no other way to reach her. I hadn't thought to ask for her number when she was here. *I was a fucking idiot!* I scolded myself, infuriated at my own goddamn stupidity. The old man mumbled something while I internally shouted, but my monologue cut off when he passed me a small piece of paper.

"She left her cell number, told me to call if I had any problems with the plane or her deliveries. You need it?"

I beamed at Joe and copied the written numbers into my satellite phone. There wasn't any cell service up here, not for miles.

I thanked Joe profusely and walked him out to the dock. He told me he'd see me next week, jumped in the cockpit, and reeled in his anchor. Within a few short minutes, he was airborne and I ran to the cabin, phone in hand. I hit "Send" on her contact information and held my breath as the phone connected, then rang. Once, twice, three times.

Pick up the damn phone, Anna!

Apparently she heard me because she picked up on the fourth ring, slightly breathless and worried. "Hello?" she asked.

All the breath whooshed out of me. Even her voice made my cock hard.

"Hello? Joe? Are you okay?"

Her anxiety ramped up and shook me from my

stupor as I quickly cleared my throat and responded. "Uh, actually it's me. Jack."

The silence on the end of the line was deafening. I waited a beat and then continued, "Joe gave me your number. He just delivered my cargo and... and it wasn't you. What the hell, princess? Why didn't you tell me you were leaving?"

I heard a small hiccup on the end of the line, like a sob but not quite. I waited for a response, but all I heard was silence.

"Damn it, Anna, talk to me!" I snapped, aware that I had lost my mind. The woman I loved was hundreds of miles away and I had no way to reach her. No way to touch her. "Are you all right? Are you okay down there? God, Anna, why didn't you tell me you were leaving?"

She stuttered a bit before she responded, "I tried to tell you, Jack, that day in your car. I'm so sorry I didn't tell you when dad's house sold. I didn't really have a way to get ahold of you, and it all happened so fast. I'm in Seattle now, I actually think I found a job." She paused for a moment before she added, "I'm really excited about this, Jack. This is what I have been dreaming about since Dad died. The house sold, I got the money, and now I'm out of Alaska. This is it, my big dream. I can't come back."

I could hear it as she bit her nails on the other end, obviously nervous about my response.

I took a moment and breathed in deeply, tried to

collect myself, and asked, "Can I come see you? I want to *see you*."

My voice broke a bit at the tension and I stopped myself before I actually *begged* her to come back to me. I heard her tiny gasp over the line and knew she was just as upset. We both sat in silence for a moment, unable to speak.

Anna finally cleared her throat and said, "Jack, I think we both know this can't go anywhere. We had fun... *so much* fun. But long distance relationships never work. And I deserve more than that."

She was right. She did. I had no right to ask her to give up her dreams for me. I had chosen a life of isolation far from civilization. But Anna had too much life in her for that. That inner fire was one of the things I loved about her.

I heard the smile in her voice, the innuendo lying just beneath the surface, but she spoke again: "And I'd be lying if I said I didn't fall for you, more than I should have. But this is *my dream*, Jack. This is a really big deal for me. There's nothing for me in Alaska, Jack. Nothing but you. And that's—"

"Not enough. I know, princess. I know." I took a staggered breath as the weight of her response settled. She had no idea that I was ready to leave the cabin and Alaska behind, that I'd talked to my cousins and was going to work with them. That I was done with my solitary confinement. I considered saying it then and there, but I held back. I didn't want to burden her with my tentative ideas and aspirations. I wanted to give her something that was real, honest and steady. That's what she was, and that was what she deserved. And so I said, "Anna, I'm so proud of you. Look at you, out of Alaska and into the Big City." I forced a smile into my voice, though it was softer than usual and tinted with sadness.

I heard the crackle of her smile, the brush of her cheek against the phone, and knew it was time to say goodbye.

"We'll talk soon, princess. Good luck with the job. I wish you nothing but the best," I told her in my best impersonation of a man whose heart wasn't actually in shards on the floor.

Again, I heard her tiny intake of breath, a small sob, before she laughed and said, "Talk to you soon, City Boy." We hung up and I walked back outside, down to the dock, and I stared out onto the water.

The lake, the trees, the mountains in the distance; they all seemed like a prison now. I felt the expanse of the space in front of me, felt the emptiness of the place beside me. I knew, even before my call with Anna, that my time in Alaska had ended. She had forced me back to life, woken up parts of me that had been dormant and hurting for too long. What I now understood was that I was in love with a tough-as-nails, independent, frustrating woman who was hell bent on living her dream. I loved Anna, I realized, because she followed her dreams out of Alaska, despite my best efforts to keep her here.

She had crafted her own life and stuck to it despite the obstacles in her path. What had I done when faced with obstacles? I had retreated into myself, to this place. I had hidden *from* reality, while Anna had run *towards* it. I turned my focus back to the cabin and decided that, while it had been a refuge for a while, it was not my reality any longer. My reality was Anna. The way her strawberry blonde hair smelled, the sound of her giggle against my neck, the fire in her eyes when we argued and talked trash. And her dreams and aspirations. All of those things were now part of my reality. I took a deep cleansing breath and stepped inside my cabin looking around, really seeing, for the first time.

Hell, there wasn't even anything here worth the time to pack.

8
———

nna

Two Months Later

I sat in the cockpit and attempted to organize the flight plan my copilot had just handed me. I noted that the flight was fairly short, just a quick jaunt over to Vancouver Island and back. The lights on the dashboard blinked comfortingly; a cockpit had always felt like home and this rig was no different. It was much nicer than my dad's old floatplane, though. The joystick didn't fall off when you pulled up, for starters. Just then, the air traffic controller crackled over my headphones and informed me that my cargo—two passengers and their luggage—were headed my way on the tarmac. We'd be all systems go in ten minutes or less.

Since I started my new job in Seattle, I had flown people, not cargo, to Vancouver Island, the San Juan Islands, and even more remote spots in Washington. It wasn't exactly what I wanted to do, but it was an amazing start.

I tallied up my flight count in my head. It wasn't as demanding as "Anna Air" was back in Alaska. I no longer loaded and unloaded cargo all day. The plane I flew was only three years old, the seats were still soft leather and the vents didn't rattle. My apartment was brand new, not a fifty year old house, complete with an indoor swimming pool, workout gym, and social events for singles on Friday nights. I bought a new car, too. She was small and cherry red. Nothing too wild, but she was all mine. I had several thousand in savings, and if this job worked out, I planned on flying to Europe the first vacation I could take. I wanted to go to France, see Paris and the Eiffel Tower and eat a croissant that melted on my tongue like flakes of butter.

I smiled at my own whimsy. I missed Jack. And when the other singles milled about down by the park, I surfed the travel websites and made my plans. It was the only way I could push down the ache in my heart caused by missing him.

After one last check of the command console, I stood in my crisp white shirt and pleated pants, hair pinned back behind my airline cap as I stared straight ahead in preparation, ready to greet my passengers.

As the first passenger came into view, I felt my heart as it thumped in my chest. The woman was tall, slender, with platinum white hair and a classic beauty about her. She smiled widely as she saw me, handed her bag to the ground crew, and reached over to hug me.

"Anna, my darling, you look just *amazing*!" she cooed as she pulled back to take me all in.

"M-Mrs. Buchanan, what are you doing here?" I finally managed to stutter out, jarred by the presence of Jack's mother. I had only met her one other time, in Anchorage when she assigned me Jack's delivery, but she was unmistakable. She had Jack's Grecian features and his no-bullshit stare.

I knew I was being rude, especially as her pilot, but my brain couldn't connect the dots. "Are you flying with us today?" I asked dumbly and immediately wanted to hit myself over the head.

"Oh, darling, did Jack not tell you? We're headed to Vancouver Island to check up on one of his father's investments. I assumed you knew when we had booked your airline! Silly Jack," she whispered conspiratorially as she winked at me. Mrs. Buchanan walked to her seat ten feet away and sat down, clearly smug and satisfied with herself.

Just then, I heard heavier steps on the plank way just outside of view. *Shit.* I just knew it was Jack. I was tempted to hide in the cockpit before he boarded, and it was only my pain-in-the-ass copilot blocking the way that stopped me. I took a deep breath and gritted my teeth. I also smoothed my hair and the front of my blouse.

My heartbeat sped to an alarming rate as Jack's shadow breached the hull of the plane and then he stepped into my line of sight. He was even more handsome now, in a beautifully cut suit with a briefcase in his masculine, rough hands. His hair had been trimmed but there was still an unmistakable, boyish wave. His brown eyes grazed up my body, then met mine.

We both stilled entirely; my face registered shock as his morphed into smug pleasure.

Jack took a step closer to me. In the small hull of the aircraft, he towered over me and blocked the aisle behind him.

"Hello, princess. Fancy seeing you here," he drawled, and his smile broke free.

His megawatt smile hit me like a ton of bricks and I couldn't help it; I smiled back. His brown eyes dropped to my smile, my lips, and then lower, to my breasts that had stood at attention the second he came through the door. Jack's eyebrows quirked up in appreciation.

I rolled my eyes but before I could slap him, Jack took both my hands in his and brought them gently to his lips. "Anna, you look... amazing. Bush pilot looked good on you, but this..." he dropped off and gestured at the full length of me, appreciating my fitted shirt, slacks, and made-up face. I blushed and dipped my head down for a moment before the steel returned to my spine, and I asked, "What are you doing here?"

The copilot called to me and I was the first to glance away.

"Thanks for coming aboard, Mr. Buchanan. If you'll take your seat, we can take off soon."

I turned numbly towards the cockpit, unsure of my ability to fly a plane while dazed and Jack-drunk.

But Jack wouldn't have it; his hands found my shoulders and he turned me to face him once again. "Anna, I didn't come here to fly with you. I came here to see you. To tell you that I miss you, and that I'm back in Seattle," he said, and he looked down at me with such intense emotion that my own eyes misted.

"What? I—" I started, but he cut me off.

"Just let me say this and then you can kick me off your plane," he pleaded. He took my lack of response as permission and continued, "The day you left the cabin, I wanted to come after you. I *should* have come after you. But I assumed you'd come back. And you didn't." Here, I tried to interject but again, he silenced me. "Shh, princess, let me finish. I assumed you'd come back, but I was wrong. I assumed that you'd stay for me, but that was idiotic of me. I was selfish and thought that you'd change your whole life for me if we wanted things to work out. I didn't give you enough credit," he finished with a huge, heart-stopping grin, an apology etched all over his face.

"What do you mean?" I asked, totally perplexed. *Credit for what?*

Jack kissed the inside of my palm and moved a step closer to me before he said, "I thought you didn't mean it when you said you'd leave. I didn't want to believe it. I hid in that cabin the second things got tough, but you fought for what you wanted and you went for it, even when you had a chance to take the easy way out."

The blush returned full force as his praise warmed me from head-to-toe. Not even my dad telling me I was a great pilot made me feel so capable, so strong. I coughed as tears threatened the back of my throat; I would *not* cry on my own damn plane.

"Damn it, Jack, a phone call wouldn't suffice?" I bit out as I blinked away moisture. My co-pilot shifted where he stood behind me, obviously listening, but I ignored him. This wasn't about him, he could just wait.

Jack's low chuckle rumbled in his chest as he stepped forward to fully embrace me. The second our chests met, the moment my head nestled under his, we both sighed. It was a contented, happy sound.

"When you left me at the cabin, I felt so alone. Like I didn't know what to do or where to go, but I knew I didn't belong there anymore. You lit a fire under my ass, princess. I worked the past couple of months with my cousins, but I still felt lost. Like I didn't have a place of refuge anymore, a place to call home. That's why I left Seattle in the first place; it stopped feeling like home. But then I met you," he finished and kissed the top if my pilot's cap. He started kissing my forehead, my cheeks, and closed in on my mouth, as if that was the end of the conversation. I pulled back, confused.

"What does meeting me have to do with finding a home?" I asked as I leaned back and met his gaze full-on.

Jack smiled sweetly at me, color flushed his face. "You are my home, Anna. Wherever you are, that's home."

I stopped breathing as tears flooded my eyes and spilled down my cheeks. "I thought you didn't want anything serious, I thought we were just—" I broke off and buried my face in his chest.

"Anna, no, we weren't *just* anything. I was an idiot and, honestly, so were you," he added with a laugh and managed to dodge my sucker punch. "But we were destined to be *more*, don't you think?"

The raw look in his eyes as his forehead met mine

undid me. I kissed him for all I was worth and forgot for a moment that I was a pilot on a plane, that the air traffic controller was talking in my headset.

I just kissed the man I loved with all I was worth... and it felt like home.

EPILOGUE

nna

Four Years Later

We sat on the edge of the lawn in our freshly-stained Adirondack chairs as the sun set behind the tree line. We roasted marshmallows, one for Julianne and one for Aaron, both of whom were too small to handle the fiery sticks themselves. Soon, we were all covered in the sticky goo from our S'mores and we laughed as Aaron, who was two and half, smeared chocolate into his hair. Jack sat on the chair with me in his lap, one of his arms banded about my waist.

The summer ended too fast, it seemed, and we were headed back to Seattle in the morning. After we got married and had Julianne, we started spending time at Jack's old cabin south of Anchorage. I flew us there, of course. Once Aaron came along, we spent full summers at the cabin and soaked up the Alaskan wilderness with our two crazy kids. Jack and I, rejuvenated by memories of our first weekend together, had tried for a third child during our stays. So far no luck, but we both agreed it was good practice.

After we wiped small fingers clean of marshmallow and cracker crumbs, the kids ran off to the porch and grabbed their moth nets. While they tried and failed to catch the moths that flew around the lampposts, Jack and I kissed each other gently in the firelight. The heat and passion of those first days had yet to dwindle with the passing years, and the cabin always stirred those embers up again. As one of Jack's hands grazed the curve of my ass and the other reached to caress my nipple, I giggled against his lips.

"Jack, the kids..." I admonished.

He turned to face the kids and shouted, "Hey kids, I'm going to kiss Mommy so don't come over here, okay?"

My jaw dropped but the kids, unfazed, just shrieked, "Ew! Gross!" and continued to play their game.

"Jack, you can't do th—" I tried to yell, but he just

kissed me harder and I stopped talking. His kiss could always shut me up and he knew it. Even after the past four years, he still turned me on and drove me crazy.

Jack broke our kiss abruptly and asked, "Can we go to bed now, princess?"

I knew he didn't mean to sleep, so I nodded and bit my lip. We held hands as we walked up to the cabin, the kids entranced by the flying moths.

"Time for bed," Jack directed and they both whined, as kids do. But they trundled into the house, down the hall, and into their bunk beds, which now took up the space that was once Jack's study. We kissed our children goodnight, and Jack's hand grazed my back sensually as I bent to tuck Aaron in tighter.

With the light turned down, we closed the door and padded to our master bedroom, Jack's hands already roaming under my shirt. I leaned against him as we shut the door, excited for a final night together in *our* cabin.

"I love you, princess," Jack whispered against the curve of my neck, and I moaned in appreciation.

"I love you, too, City Boy," I responded and was rewarded with his low belly laugh.

We fell into bed together, laughter on our lips and so much love between us.

———

Ready for more? Read A Bargain with the Billionaire **next!**

She thinks I'm too young. She's wrong. I can give her what she wants. A baby.

It will be my pleasure. And hers.

But only if she'll give me the one thing I need…HER.

Click here to read A Bargain with the Billionaire **now!**

GET A FREE BOOK!

Join my mailing list to be the first to know of new releases, free books, special prices and other author giveaways.

http://freehotcontemporary.com

ALSO BY JESSA JAMES

Bad Boy Billionaires

A Virgin for the Billionaire

Her Rockstar Billionaire

Her Secret Billionaire

A Bargain with the Billionaire

Billionaire Box Set 1-4

The Virgin Pact

The Teacher and the Virgin

His Virgin Nanny

His Dirty Virgin

The Virgin Pact Boxed Set

Club V

Unravel

Undone

Uncover

Club V - The Complete Boxed Set

Cowboy Romance

How To Love A Cowboy

How To Hold A Cowboy

Treasure: The Series

Capture

Control

Bad Behavior

Bad Reputation

Bad Behavior/Bad Reputation Duet

Beg Me

Valentine Ever After

Covet/Crave

Kiss Me Again

Contemporary Heat Boxed Set 1

Handy

Dr. Hottie

Hot as Hell

Contemporary Heat Boxed Set 2

Pretend I'm Yours

Rock Star

The Baby Mission

ABOUT THE AUTHOR

Jessa James grew up on the East Coast but always suffered a severe case of wanderlust. She's lived in six states, had a variety of jobs and always comes back to her first true love – writing. Jessa works full time as a writer, eats too much dark chocolate, has an iced-coffee and Cheetos addiction, and can't get enough of sexy alpha males who know exactly what they want – and aren't afraid to say it. Dominant, alpha-male insta-luv is her favorite to read (and write).

Sign up HERE for Jessa's Newsletter:

http://jessajamesauthor.com/mailing-list/

www.ingramcontent.com/pod-product-compliance
Lightning Source LLC
LaVergne TN
LVHW011848060526
838200LV00054B/4231